Dear Parents:

Congratulations! Your child is taking the first steps on an exciting journey. The destination? Independent reading!

STEP INTO READING® will help your child get there. The program offers five steps to reading success. Each step includes fun stories and colorful art or photographs. In addition to original fiction and books with favorite characters, there are Step into Reading Non-Fiction Readers, Phonics Readers and Boxed Sets, Sticker Readers, and Comic Readers—a complete literacy program with something to interest every child.

Learning to Read, Step by Step!

Ready to Read Preschool–Kindergarten
• big type and easy words • rhyme and rhythm • picture clues
For children who know the alphabet and are eager to begin reading.

Reading with Help Preschool–Grade 1
• basic vocabulary • short sentences • simple stories
For children who recognize familiar words and sound out new words with help.

Reading on Your Own Grades 1–3
• engaging characters • easy-to-follow plots • popular topics
For children who are ready to read on their own.

Reading Paragraphs Grades 2–3
• challenging vocabulary • short paragraphs • exciting stories
For newly independent readers who read simple sentences with confidence.

Ready for Chapters Grades 2–4
• chapters • longer paragraphs • full-color art
For children who want to take the plunge into chapter books but still like colorful pictures.

STEP INTO READING® is designed to give every child a successful reading experience. The grade levels are only guides; children will progress through the steps at their own speed, developing confidence in their reading.

Remember, a lifetime love of reading starts with a single step!

Published in the United States by Random House Children's Books, a division of Penguin
Random House LLC, 1745 Broadway, New York, NY 10019, and in Canada by Penguin Random
House Canada Limited, Toronto.

Step into Reading, Random House, and the Random House colophon are registered trademarks
of Penguin Random House LLC.

Visit us on the Web!
StepIntoReading.com
rhcbooks.com

Educators and librarians, for a variety of teaching tools, visit us at RHTeachersLibrarians.com

ISBN 978-0-593-12212-9 (trade) — ISBN 978-0-593-12213-6 (lib. bdg.)
ISBN 978-0-593-12214-3 (ebook)

Printed in the United States of America   10 9 8 7 6 5 4 3 2 1

WONDER WOMAN™

Three Big Bullies!

by Christy Webster

illustrated by Pernille Ørum

Wonder Woman created by
William Moulton Marston

Random House 🏠 New York

Wonder Woman is
a hero.
She helps people
every day.

Giganta is an evil
scientist.

She does not help people.

She only thinks
of herself.

Giganta makes a serum.
It makes her grow
and grow and grow!

The sorceress Circe
uses her powerful magic
to do bad deeds.

The Cheetah

is a fierce villain.

These villains want

to rule the city,

but Wonder Woman
always stops them.
Even as a giant,
Giganta cannot win.
Unless . . .

Giganta's big size gives Circe an idea. She uses her magic on herself and the Cheetah. Now there are *three* giants!

The villains
take over
the city square.
They act like big bullies.
All the people
are frightened!

The three villains
are very *big*.
Wonder Woman is small,
but she is not afraid.

Wonder Woman
has an idea.
What if she got
big, too?
The TV news crew has
just what she needs!

"STOP!"

Wonder Woman is big!

The huge pictures
of Wonder Woman
distract the bullies
for a moment.
It is just enough time
for the hero to get
the people to safety!

Wonder Woman quickly
gets everyone
into a subway station.

The bullies have

no one to bully.

Wonder Woman makes everyone feel safe. They see that all the fun is underground!

The villains are bored.
They do not want
to take over a city
with no people in it.
Giganta, Circe,
and the Cheetah shrink
to their regular sizes
so they can go into
the subway station, too.

The bullies charge in!
They do not want
the people
to have any fun.

Wonder Woman stops
the villains
with her lasso.
Everyone else celebrates!

The police take
the villains away.
The city square
is safe again.

Wonder Woman has saved the day! You don't have to be big to be brave.